THE DINOSAUR THAT POOPED A PLANET!

Check out Danny and Dinosaur in more adventures:
THE DINOSAUR THAT POOPED CHRISTMAS
THE DINOSAUR THAT POOPED THE PAST!
THE DINOSAUR THAT POOPED SPACE: STICKER ACTIVITY BOOK
THE DINOSAUR THAT POOPED A PLANET: SOUND BOOK
THE DINOSAUR THAT POOPED A LOT!
THE DINOSAUR THAT POOPED THE BED!

To Danny & Harry, the most flatulent people we know – T.F. & D.P.
For Codie – G.P.

THE DINOSAUR THAT POOPED A PLANET!
A RED FOX BOOK 978 1 849 41808 9

Published in Great Britain by Red Fox,
an imprint of Random House Children's Publishers UK
A Penguin Random House Company

This edition published 2013

3 5 7 9 10 8 6 4

Copyright © Tom Fletcher and Dougie Poynter, 2013
Illustrated by Garry Parsons

The right of Tom Fletcher, Dougie Poynter and Garry Parsons to be identified as the authors and illustrator
of this work has been asserted in accordance with the Copyright, Designs and Patents Act 1988.
All rights reserved. No part of this publication may be reproduced, stored in a retrieval system,
or transmitted in any form or by any means, electronic, mechanical, photocopying, recording
or otherwise, without the prior permission of the publishers.

Red Fox Books are published by Random House Children's Publishers UK,
61–63 Uxbridge Road, London W5 5SA

www.**randomhousechildrens**.co.uk
www.**totallyrandombooks**.co.uk
www.**randomhouse**.co.uk

Addresses for companies within The Random House Group Limited
can be found at: www.**randomhouse**.co.uk/offices.htm
THE RANDOM HOUSE GROUP Limited Reg. No. 954009
A CIP catalogue record for this book is available from the British Library.

Printed in China

MIX
Paper from
responsible sources
FSC® C018179

Penguin Random House is committed to a
sustainable future for our business, our readers
and our planet. This book is made from Forest
Stewardship Council® certified paper.

THE DINOSAUR THAT POOPED A PLANET!

Tom Fletcher and Dougie Poynter
Illustrated by Garry Parsons

RED FOX

Danny and Dinosaur liked to have fun.
Some days they had lots, some days they had none.

One day they were bored, they had no games to play.
Danny said, "Dinosaur, what shall we do today?
We could mow the lawn. We could tidy the place.
We could do our chores or we could go to space!"

"But you mustn't forget to have lunch," said their mummy.
"You cannot have fun without food for your tummy."
So they packed a packed lunch for the Science Museum,
Where rockets were kept if you wanted to see them.

There were hundreds of rockets and spaceship surprises,
Tall ones and small ones of all shapes and sizes.
And one that was ready to launch, with a door
Big enough for a boy and his pet dinosaur.

They ignored all the warnings – they couldn't care less.
They pressed all the things they shouldn't have pressed.

T-minus 5 4 3 2 1 IGNITION!

They started their intergalactic space mission.

They flew higher than houses,
and buildings, and cranes;
Much higher than birds,
even higher than planes.

"We're in space!" Danny yelled as they floated around.
But the dinosaur's tum made a rumbling sound.

"Is it time to have lunch?" Danny looked at his watch.
   Then he looked all around for the dino's lunchbox.
Danny started to worry, then started to panic . . .
   They'd left their packed lunches back home on their planet!

So with no food on board, not the smallest of crumbs,
A disastrous dinosaur feast had begun!

It gobbled up gadgets and gizmos galore –
    Nothing was safe from the space dinosaur.
Robots and ray guns and blinking red blinkers,
    Eating things thought up by NASA's great thinkers!
The hyperdrive-gamma-reactor-machine
    Was swallowed along with the space tractor beam.

It chewed and it chomped on the spaceship controls –
The rocket was dotted with dino tooth holes!
Inside it was bare, the spaceship was empty.
Outside there were more things to eat – there was plenty!

It broke down the door
with a cool ninja chop!
Out in space dinosaurs are
much harder to stop.

It chomped on the moon like a big chunk of cheese,
Then shoved even more in its mouth with a squeeze.

It munched on the Martians from Mars and their cats
　　(Their cats are like ours, but their cats wear cool hats),
Satellites, Saturn and six supernovas,
　　Shapeshifting saucers and seven space rovers.

It guzzled five gallons of fuel from the tank,
  And Danny's jaw dropped as he watched what it drank!
With a crunch and a crack and a nom-nom-nom-nom,
  In one dino gulp, their rocket was gone!

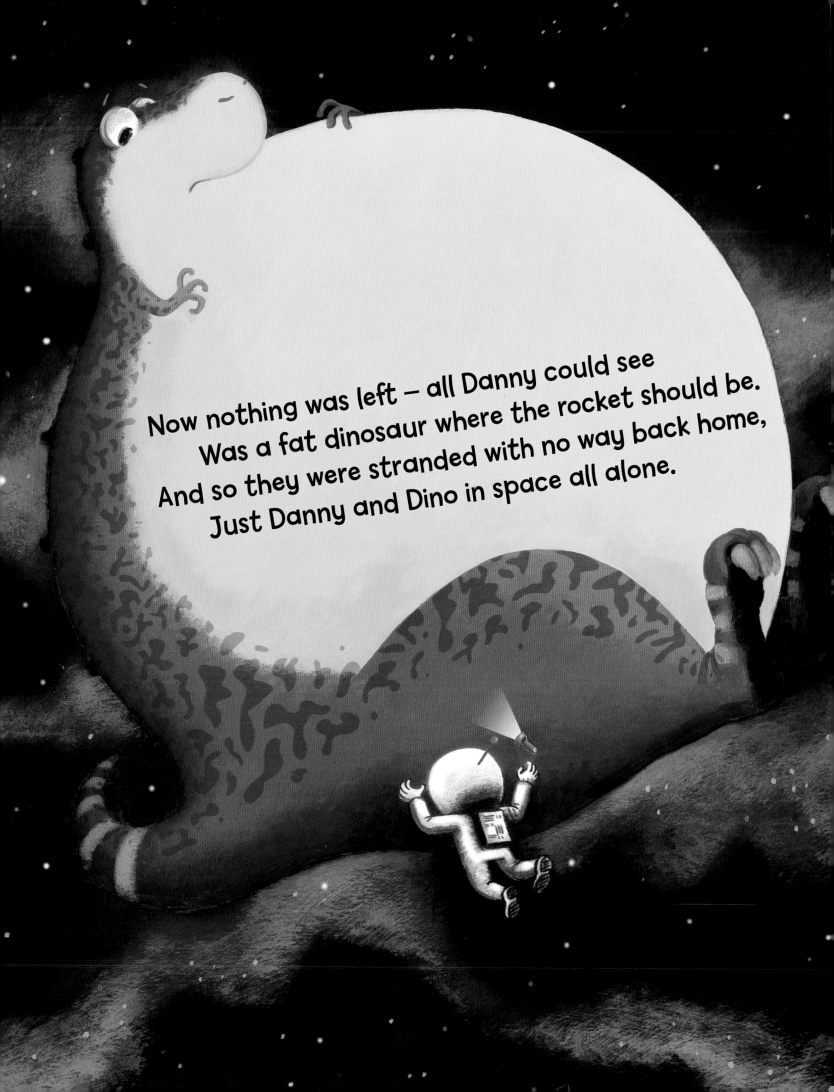

Now nothing was left – all Danny could see
Was a fat dinosaur where the rocket should be.
And so they were stranded with no way back home,
Just Danny and Dino in space all alone.

Now Danny was crying,

He cried
and he cried,

He cried and his
tears filled his
space suit inside.

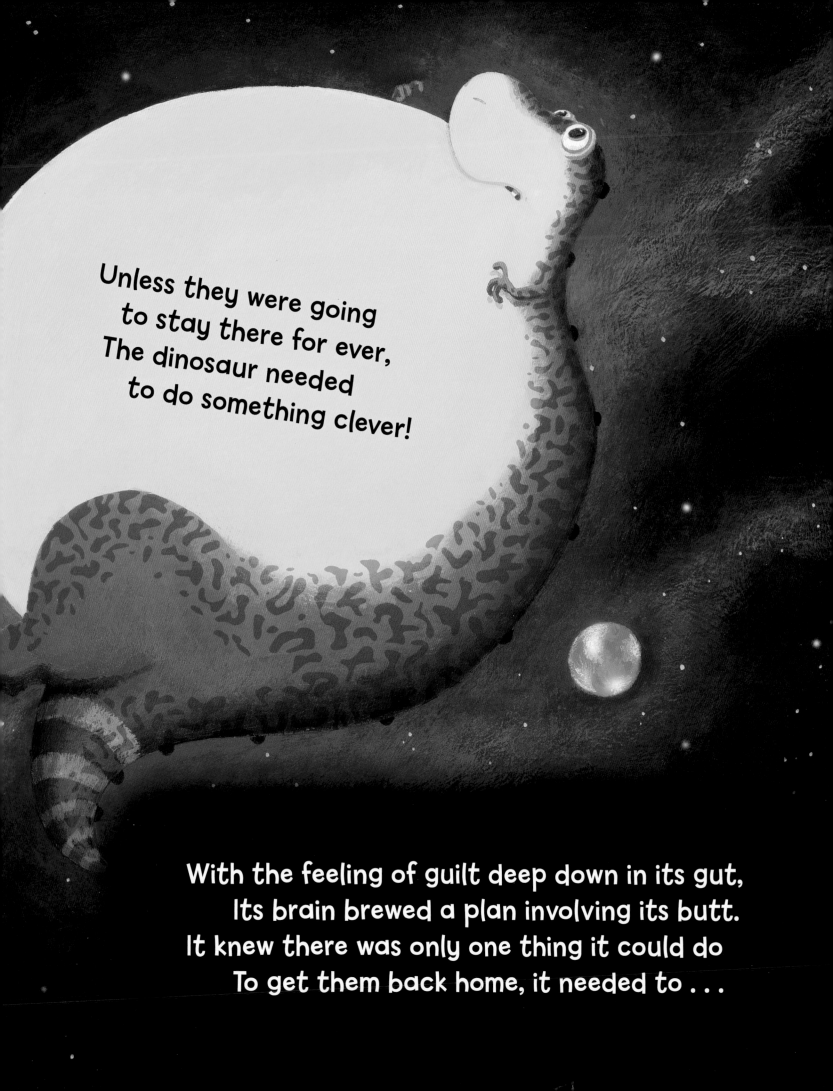

Unless they were going
to stay there for ever,
The dinosaur needed
to do something clever!

With the feeling of guilt deep down in its gut,
Its brain brewed a plan involving its butt.
It knew there was only one thing it could do
To get them back home, it needed to . . .

Like a poop-powered rocket the dinosaur flew.
   Dan hopped on its back and he watched as it pooed.
It pooped out the robots and ray guns and blinkers –
   The things NASA's thinkers thought up were now stinkers!
It pooped out the moon, it pooped out the stars,
   It pooped the space rovers and Martians from Mars.

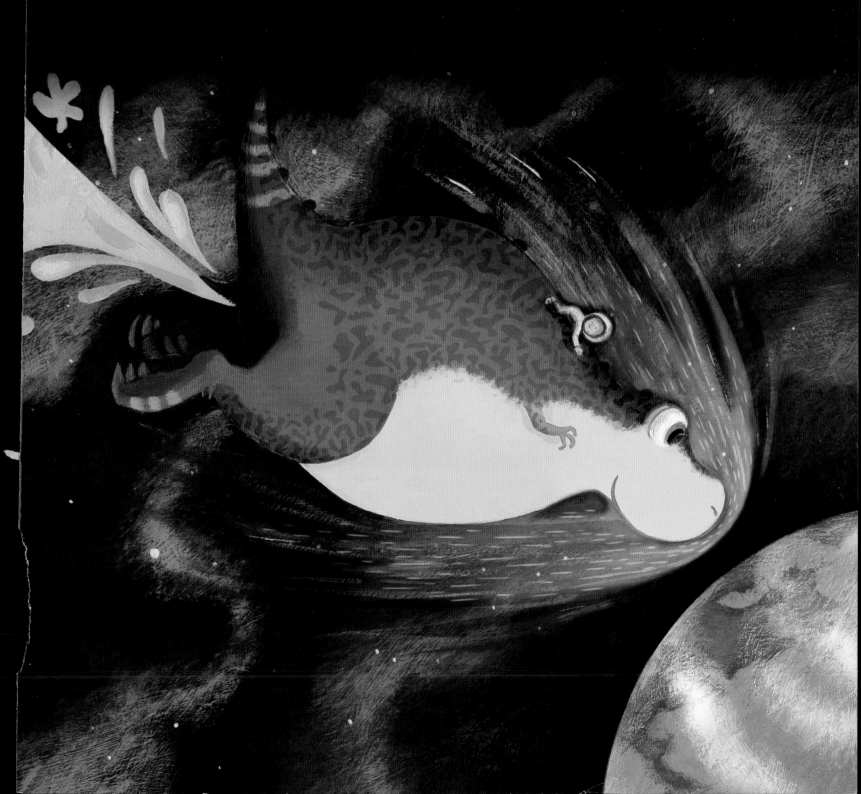

When Danny looked back he could see a poop trail
From far out in space to the dinosaur's tail.
They headed for Earth and they started to orbit.
It pooped on the clouds,
but the clouds just absorbed it.

They flew past the buildings and streets of their town,
Leaving the houses all smelly and brown,
And finally landed back down on the ground.
"Hooray!" Danny cried. "We are home, safe and sound!"

They looked to the sky, and the things that were pooed
Had formed a poop planet right next to the moon.
And so Danny promised to listen to Mummy,
Because fun is not fun without food for your tummy.

. . . and just when you thought all the pooping was done,
a Mars cat plopped out of the dinosaur's bum.